Copyright © 2021 La'Tosha Price

ISBN: 9798825525730

Imprint: Independently published

Published by: La'Tosha Price

Pricelessstorytime@gmail.com

Edited by: Pastor Carlos Price

Illustrated by: La'Tosha Price

tosharp@gmail.com

I

Introduction

I'm a creator, a visionary, a playwright and a storyteller. I approach the world with the eyes of an artist, the ears of a musician, and the soul of a writer. I see the endless possibilities when others see only problems and obstacles. Musical plays, children's art museums, and my own children have been sources of inspiration to me, as well as gospel music and praise and worship. I value the importance of abandoning momentarily my adult wisdom and knowledge so that I can accurately tell a story about life through a child's eyes. I believe that quality is one of God's gifts to me.

Another of His gifts to me is writing. I love to write! Maybe that's because words flow easily from my brain to my fingertips, and my heart beats rapidly with excitement as my efforts allow an idea to become a reality on the paper in front of me. No matter the time of night or day that I sit to focus upon writing, once the story is inside me, I have to tell it! If my family members are nearby, they must hear about what I'm thinking. And then the magic happens when I assume the mind of a child and present my story in written form.

All children delight in reading stories about characters looking and acting like they do. However, for reasons of history, racism, economics and so much more, there are too few children's books where African-American kids like mine get to feel validated by the content of the stories they read. I felt compelled to take action by using my gifts to honor God and children together. So this book about a series of events in the life of "Jazzy Jada'" details incidences that happen to all children, but the faces of all the characters here are of persons of color.

My goal is to spread the word about the power of accomplishing your dreams, and the excellence in reading that produces the power of knowledge! I learned to dream through reading, learned to create dreams through writing, and learned to develop dreamers through teaching. I shall always be a dreamer. Dreams really do come true, so I invite readers to come along and dream.

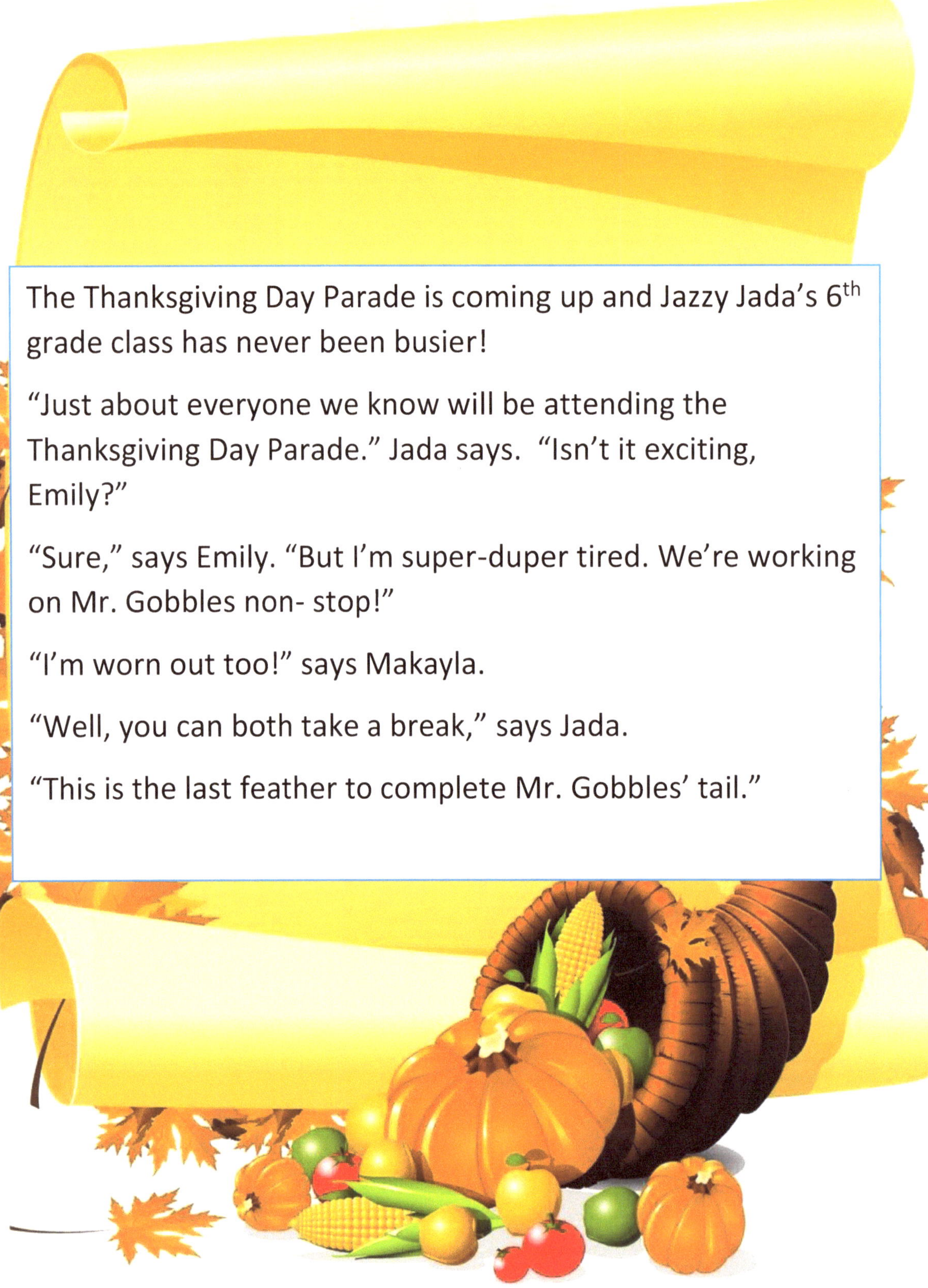

The Thanksgiving Day Parade is coming up and Jazzy Jada's 6th grade class has never been busier!

"Just about everyone we know will be attending the Thanksgiving Day Parade." Jada says. "Isn't it exciting, Emily?"

"Sure," says Emily. "But I'm super-duper tired. We're working on Mr. Gobbles non- stop!"

"I'm worn out too!" says Makayla.

"Well, you can both take a break," says Jada.

"This is the last feather to complete Mr. Gobbles' tail."

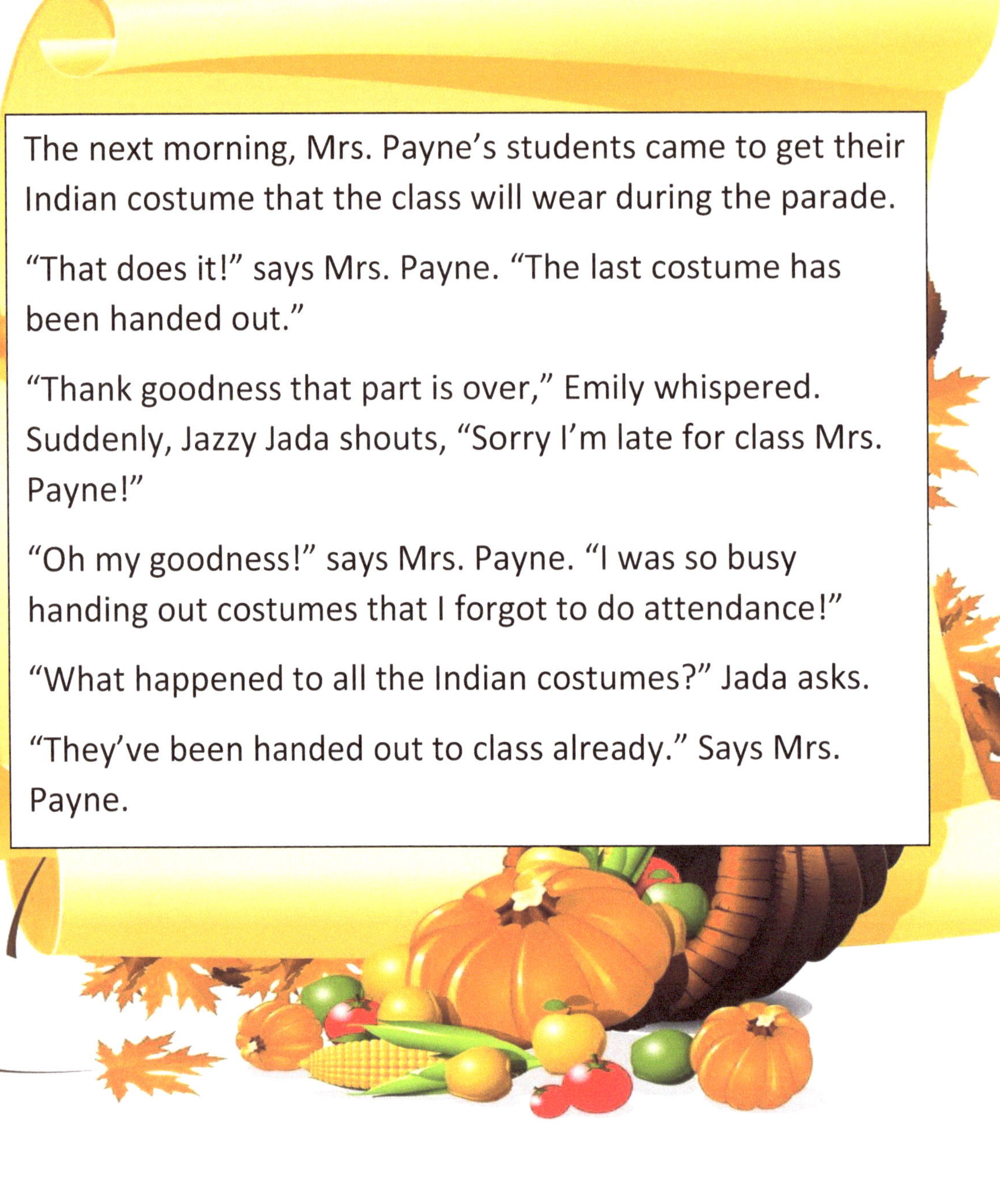

The next morning, Mrs. Payne's students came to get their Indian costume that the class will wear during the parade.

"That does it!" says Mrs. Payne. "The last costume has been handed out."

"Thank goodness that part is over," Emily whispered. Suddenly, Jazzy Jada shouts, "Sorry I'm late for class Mrs. Payne!"

"Oh my goodness!" says Mrs. Payne. "I was so busy handing out costumes that I forgot to do attendance!"

"What happened to all the Indian costumes?" Jada asks.

"They've been handed out to class already." Says Mrs. Payne.

Mrs. Payne
6th Grade Class

"No, Mrs. Payne," Jada says. "I totally forgot all about it while working to add the last touches to Mr. Gobbles."

"We only have one costume left. The Indiana Chief," Mrs. Payne says.

"But, Mrs. Payne," Jada whispered. "That's a boy's costume isn't it?" "Yes," says Mrs. Payne. "Oh," says Jazzy Jada. "I'm not feeling too cute in boy's clothing."

Emily covers her eyes. "I can't bear to watch this."

"And this big hat is way too big for my head." Jazzy Jada says.

"Thank goodness she's not going to wear that." says Makayla.

"I guess that's the price you pay for being late to class," whimpers Jada. "Don't worry, Jada," says Emily.

 "We can make you a hat for the costume. You will be the best girl Indian Chief ever seen!"

"Really?" says Jazzy Jada. "Thank you so much. Let's get started."

Mrs. Payne
Grade Class

But when the girls got to the art room they find that their all out of supplies.

"I'm sure we can find enough odds and ends around our houses," Emily suggested.

The girls hop on their bikes and head to Emily's house first.

"You can use my stretchy head band," says Emily.

"Look you can use my mom's old feather duster for the feathers." Makayla added.

Emily's mother helps too! She brings seashells and gives Jada a colorful ribbon.

Before long, Jazzy Jada's Indian Chief Hat took shape.

"Now, all done. Let's get back home and eat some pizza and finish our homework," Jazzy Jada says.

"It's getting late and we have to prepare the float early in the morning for the parade."

The next morning, Makayla and Emily can't find Jazzy Jada's Indian Chief Hat anywhere!

"Maybe Jada came and got it early this morning," says Emily.

"Look!" shouted Makayla. "Someone dropped one of the feathers on the floor!"

"Oh, no!" cries Emily. "Jada will be here any minute!"

"We have to act fast. What are we going to tell her?" asked Makayla.

"Hurry! Grab whatever we can find from the art room", yelled Emily. "We have to make a new hat."

The girls raced from classroom to classroom grabbing anything they could find.

Mrs. Payne
6th Grade Class

Just then, Jazzy Jada comes through the art classroom door.

"Here's your hat," Emily says slowly.

"Oh my goodness, what happened to the hat we worked on all last night!" asked Jazzy Jada.

"We have no idea," Makayla mutters.

Jada reaches for the new hat and tries it on. "Why, its' too big!"

"Why would anyone want to take that hat?" Makayla asked the girls.

"I'm not sure, but I am going to get to the bottom of this!" shouted Jazzy Jada.

Mrs. Payne
6th Grade Class

The girls followed the feathers out the door and down hall. Around the corner to the nurse's office across the walkway and down the stairs, near the library and ended at the gym's wooden doors.

"The hat has to be in there," explained Jazzy Jada.

The girls opened the door and there in all its beauty was none other than Mr. Gobbles.

"Mr. Gobbles took my hat?" Jazzy Jada asked.

"That's what it looks like, but how?" Makayla asked.

Just then Mrs. Payne came over to meet us. "Why, it wonderful! Says Mrs. Payne.

The girls looked very puzzled. "What's wonderful?" they asked.

"Why the hat for Mr. Gobbles it's the perfect finishing touch!" says Mrs. Payne.

EXIT

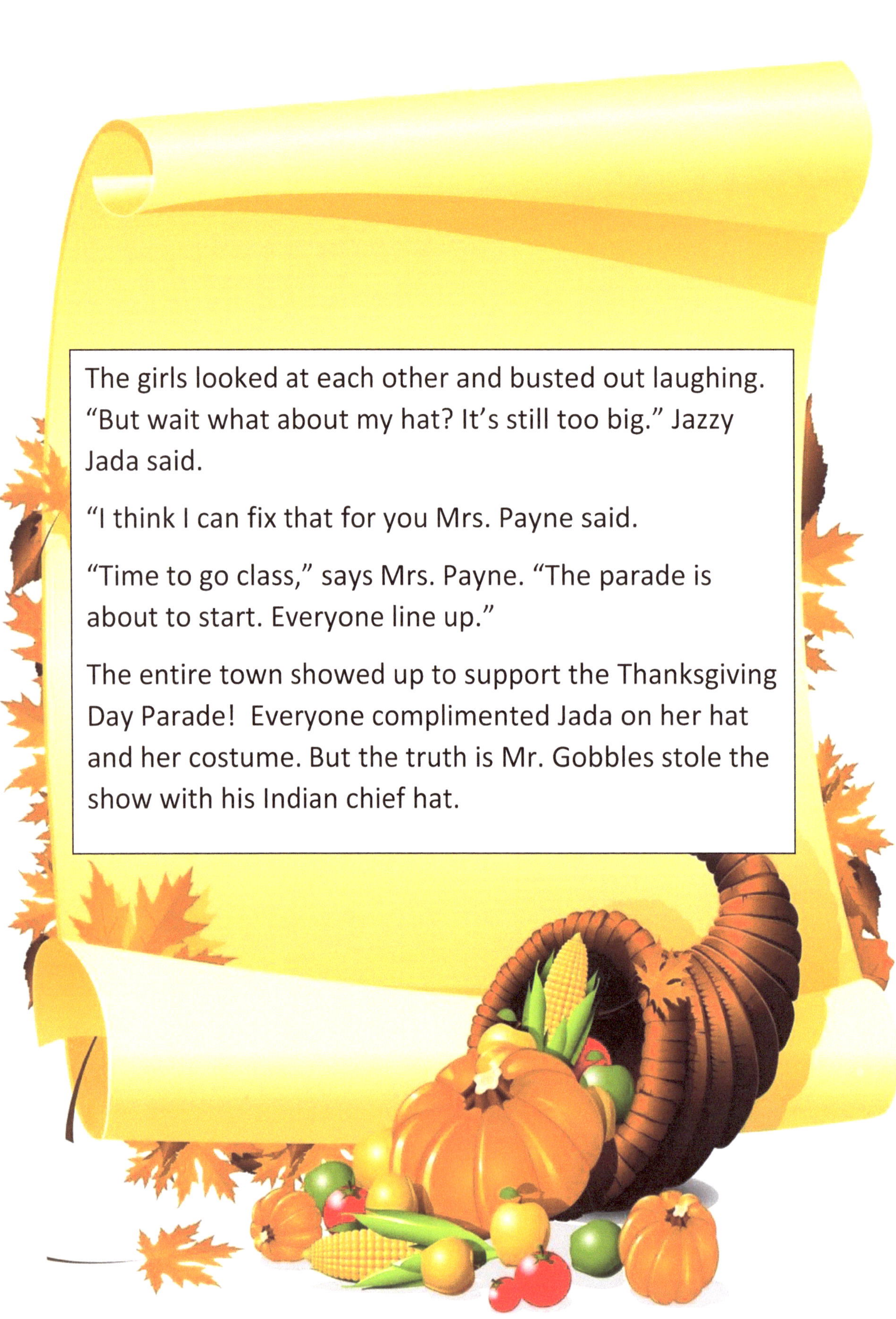

The girls looked at each other and busted out laughing. "But wait what about my hat? It's still too big." Jazzy Jada said.

"I think I can fix that for you Mrs. Payne said.

"Time to go class," says Mrs. Payne. "The parade is about to start. Everyone line up."

The entire town showed up to support the Thanksgiving Day Parade! Everyone complimented Jada on her hat and her costume. But the truth is Mr. Gobbles stole the show with his Indian chief hat.

Happy Thanksgiving

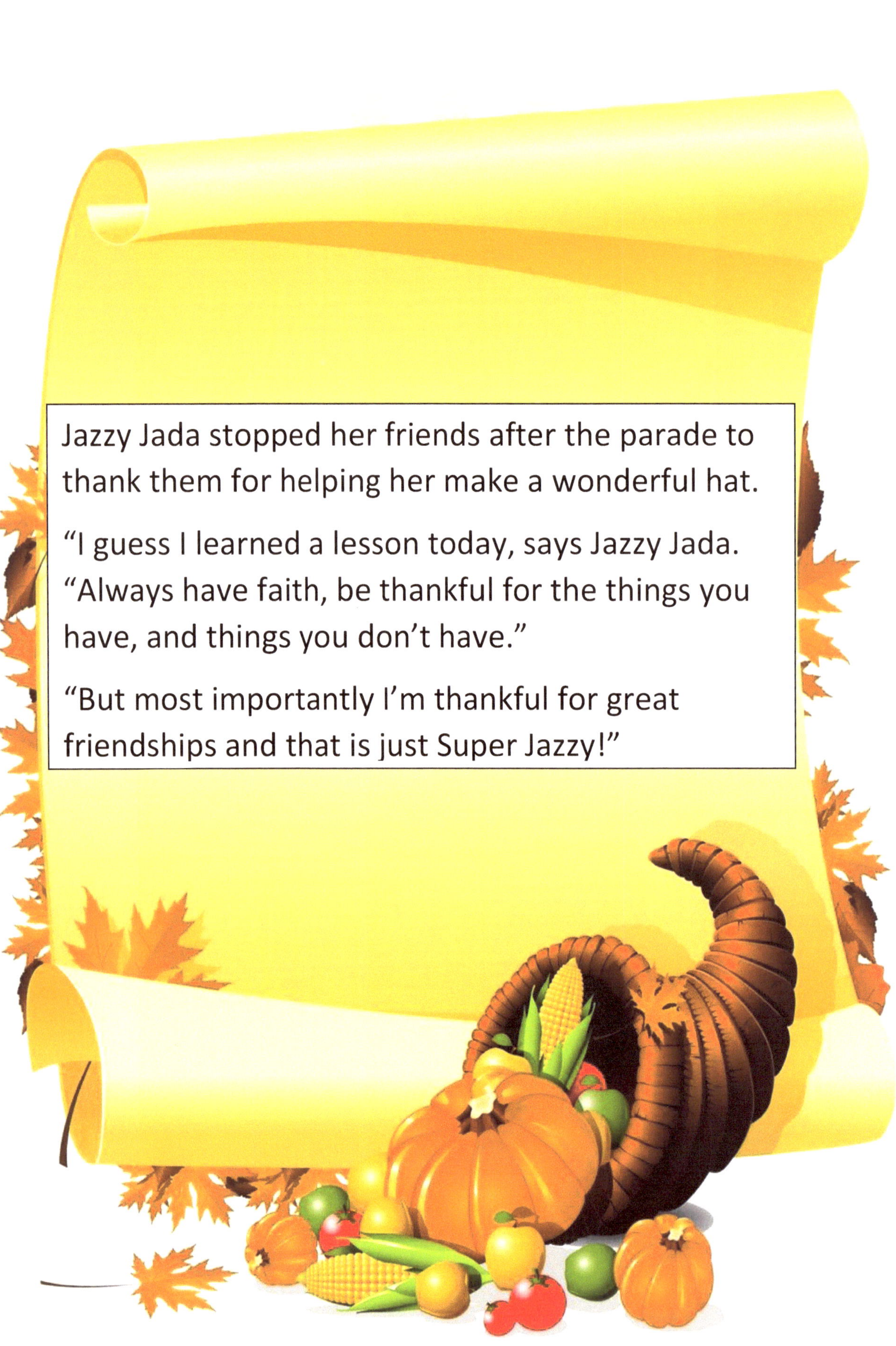

Jazzy Jada stopped her friends after the parade to thank them for helping her make a wonderful hat.

"I guess I learned a lesson today, says Jazzy Jada. "Always have faith, be thankful for the things you have, and things you don't have."

"But most importantly I'm thankful for great friendships and that is just Super Jazzy!"

 Up and coming author, La'Tosha Price welcomed her new character "Jazzy Jada" in her beloved children's book, Jazz It up with Jazzy Jada. Now with a new spin her character "Jazzy Jada" is growing up fast. La'Tosha was inspired by her daughter, Jada, who was six years JAZZY old and begging to receive an African- American doll for Christmas. After making futile searches, La' Tosha realized she needed to create what her JADA daughter, and all little girls of color needed badly —to see herself as the center of her young world. "Jazzy Jada" came into existence.

Jazzy Jada is an African-American five-year-old girl whose daily experiences are filled with "jazzy" laughter and life's lessons. Her first book contains five stories: Jazzy Jada's Pink Scooter and The Black Bandits teach her not to always believe what others say. Jazzy Jada Takes A Sick Day has a twist of truth at the end and teaches Jada to always tell the truth. The Great Baby Escape is about responsibility and babysitting. Jazzy Jada and Tea With A Queen teaches her to be gracious in all circumstances. And Jazzy Jada Goes to Kindergarten explores every child's emotions transitioning from home to school.

Jazzy Jada's newest book *"Jazzy Jada and The Thanksgiving Day Parade",* is her greatest adventure yet: The Thanksgiving Day Parade show how Jada shares her love for her friends and what it means to work hard. *"Jazzy Jada and the Thanksgiving Day parade"*, is a classic friendship story about coming together in hard time and supporting one another. Come along and enjoy this book that will delight young readers everywhere, particularly African-American girls. This fun-filled book will leave your young readers wanting to read every single story that's part of the series Jazzy Jada Is Growing Up!

 La'Tosha Price is a professional medical vendor consultant. She's a native of Bardstown, Kentucky, married to Carlos Price for twenty-one blissful years, and the proud mother of three daughters and one son. She's also a grandmother. La' Tosha has been honored with the Positive Leadership Award, the Dean's Award from Spencerian College, and the President's Club Award from Beta Sigma Chi Chapter. In her youth, she won a Young Leader Writing Award, had her story featured on the front page of the Bardstown newspaper, and received an honorary trip to South Carolina with co-writer Cabrina Logan of Bardstown Kentucky.

La' Tosha and husband Carlos are Assistant Pastors at Faith Convent Fellowship Church of Winter Park, FL under the direction of Bishop Barry Brandon. When La' Tosha is not working, she loves to write, swim, participate in theatrical arts, and go bike riding. She and her family reside in Kissimmee, Florida.

Other Books by Author

On Amazon

Awesome
Aspyn Counts
To 12!!
Written By La'Tosha Price

www.ingramcontent.com/pod-product-compliance
Lightning Source LLC
Chambersburg PA
CBHW042133110726
48006CB00003B/866